PAPERCUT⚡™

New York

TABLE OF CONTENTS

NICKELODEON BREADWINNERS

JOURNEY to the Bottom of the Seats

"LOTSA TOTS"
Stefan Petrucha – Writer
Allison Strejlau – Artist
Laurie E. Smith – Colorist
Tom Orzechowski – Letterer

"JOURNEY TO THE BOTTOM OF THE SEATS"
Stefan Petrucha – Writer
Mike Kazaleh – Artist
Laurie E. Smith – Colorist
Tom Orzechowski – Letterer

"CLOWN DOWN"
Stefan Petrucha – Writer
Allison Strejlau – Artist
Laurie E. Smith – Colorist
Tom Orzechowski – Letterer

"MISSION SUSPICION"
Stefan Petrucha – Writer
Allison Strejlau – Artist
Laurie E. Smith – Colorist
Tom Orzechowski – Letterer

Based on the Nickelodeon animated
TV series created by
Gary "Doodles" DiRaffeale and Steve Borst.

Chris Nelson – Design/Production
James Salerno – Sr. Art Director/Nickelodeon
Jeff Whitman – Production Coordinator
Bethany Bryan, Suzannah Rowntree, Michael Petranek – Editors
Joan Hilty – Comics Editor/Nickelodeon
Dan Berlin, Dani Breckenridge – Editorial Interns
Jim Salicrup
Editor-in-Chief

ISBN: 978-1-62991-300-1 paperback edition
ISBN: 978-1-62991-301-8 hardcover edition

Printed in the USA through
Four Colour Print Group
November 2015 by Lifetouch Printing
5126 Forest Hills Ct., Loves Park, IL 61111

Distributed by Macmillan
First Printing

THIS IS IT, OLD BUDDY! WE'RE *TOAST!*

WE ONLY HAVE SECONDS LEFT, BEST FRIEND!

ONE HOUR LATER...

OH.

SHE LAID A BUNCH OF EGGS.

HUH, THIS ISN'T SO BAD!

WEAGGGGGGHH!

POP POP POP POP POP POP POP

DON'T THINK I DON'T SEE *YOU*, TOO!

I'LL ALSO HAVE YOU KNOW THIS IS A *NO SITTING ZONE!*

RRR?

RAAARRRGHHH!

⇒EEP⇒

SWAYSWAY, THEY'RE NOT CLEANING UP EASY! WHAT DO WE DO?

PIP.

FIRT.

⇒URG!⇒ WHAT DO YOU DO WITH *ANY* BABY, BUHDEUCE?

KOOP.

BOT.

14

I... UH... WHAT...?

DON'T WORRY! AS A PRIZED CUSTOMER, YOU'RE COVERED BY OUR NEW *NO-LASTING-DAMAGE* CLAUSE! WE'LL HAVE THIS PLACE CLEANED UP IN NO TIME!

SORRY FOR ANY INCONVEN-IENCE!

SOON...

YOU TAKE CARE NOW!

UH...

ZOT?

OH, MY.

BRAAAAAAF

THE END.

NOOOOO! ANYTHING BUT *THAT*!

THIS ISN'T A DREAM... IT'S A *NIGHTMARE*!

WAIT...

WHAT'S THIS?

⇒GASP!⇐ MY OLD P-P-PENCIL? THE ONE I ⇒SOB⇐ LOGGED MY *FIRST* BREAD DELIVERY WITH?

I MISSED YOU *SO* MUCH!

WELL PLUCK MY FEATHERS AND PREHEAT THE OVEN! MAYBE TAKING APART THE VAN WON'T BE *SO* BAD!

MAYBE IT'LL BE...

AN ADVENTURE INTO THE PAST!

WITH *ACE DUCK EXPLORER*, SWAYSWAY!

AND HIS *LOYAL GUIDE*, ME!

KETTA'S DONE HER PART, IT'S UP TO US!

YOU GOT THAT RIGHT! I'M GOING TO GO GRAB A FRUIT DRINK. WANT ONE?

NOT RIGHT NOW, THANKS.

IT'S TIME TO *LUH*-LUH-LUH-LUH...

LEVEL UP!

ACTION HERO DUCKS!

NINJA ROLL!

CARTWHEEL!

SOMERSAULT!

FLIP!

31

I'VE GOT AN IDEA OF HOW TO GET *RID* OF THOSE RATS, MY *DUCKY-DUCK*. FIRST, WE GOTTA SNEAK BACK IN THERE!

BUT WE JUST *LEFT!*

I JUST NEEDED TO BUY US TIME TO THINK.

FIRST WE GRAB A FEW LOAVES OF OUR DELICIOUS *CLAMMY BRIOCHE* BREAD.

NEXT, WE LEAVE A TRAIL OF *CRUMBS* WITH A SPECIAL *AROMA* THAT NO SELF-RESPECTING RAT CAN RESIST!

IS IT ME OR DOES ANYONE SMELL... *CHEESE* WITH A HINT OF CLAM SAUCE?

SNIFF
SNIFF

TANTILIZING AROMA

STAY IN LINE! THIS ISN'T A RAT RACE!

NO, WAIT. OF COURSE IT IS! NEVER MIND.

WHILE YOU WERE DOING YOUR VERMIN DEALING, I PUT THE ROCKET VAN BACK TOGETHER! SHE'S GOOD AS NEW, EXCEPT FOR ALL THESE LEFT OVER PIECES!

YOU KNOW WHAT *THAT* MEANS!

DO I?!

VROOOOOM

WOOHOO!

YEAH, BOYEEEE!

VROOOOOM

YOU KNOW, THIS SEEMS *FAMILIAR!* ARE WE IN OUR OWN RAT-RUT?

WHO CARES?! IT'S FUNKY FEATHERY FUN!

AND WE'LL *NEVER* BE LIKE THOSE SILLY RATS, WALKING IN CIRCLES, DOING THE SAME THING OVER AND OVER!

WE'RE GONNA MAKE IT! I *KNOW* WE...

BUBBLE NUGGETS!

LOOK AT THAT, THEY'RE *STILL* AT IT.

NEVER GIVE UP! NEVER SURRENDER!

MAYBE THEY'RE *NOT* SO STUPID. AFTER ALL, OUR BREAD IS *THAT* GOOD NO MATTER HOW MUCH YOU EAT!

AND *I'M* STARTING TO *LIKE* CRASHING THE VAN!

THE END

WATCH OUT FOR PAPERCUTZ

Welcome to the fabulous, fat-free, fast-paced, first **BREADWINNERS** graphic novel from Papercutz—those hard-working, enthusiastic, comic-makers dedicated to publishing graphic novels for all ages. I'm Jim Salicrup, the carb-loving Editor-in-Chief, and I'm here to bring you up to speed on what we have planned for the future—and beyond! But as I was writing this page, I suddenly had a touch of déjà vu and realized I said much of this already in our first **SANJAY AND CRAIG** graphic novel (still on sale wherever awesome graphic novels are sold!). So, rather than find a clever way to say everything all over again with different words, I'll just take the easy way out and use most of the same words!

Let's start at the beginning. A little over ten years ago, Papercutz publisher Terry Nantier and I founded this little comicbook company to address a need—there just didn't seem to be enough comics and graphic novels for kids. That was incredibly ironic, since most folks think of comics as being for kids. After ten years of producing all types of comics for all ages, we made an incredible deal with the awesome folks at Nickelodeon to create a line of graphic novels based on their latest and greatest new animated series. This really is a match made in cartoon heaven – Nickelodeon, loved by millions of kids for their brilliant cartoon shows and characters, and Papercutz, the graphic novel publisher devoted to creating the best comics for kids—together at last!

Terry and I, along with Joan Hilty and Linda Lee, got to spend a day at the Nickelodeon Animation Studio where we talked about our plans with the creators of Sanjay and Craig, Breadwinners, and more. Everyone was excited and as thrilled as we were about the characters leaping off the TV screen and onto the comicbook page!

To kick off this historic publishing partnership, we launched an all-new **NICKELODEON MAGAZINE**, which, in addition to features such as posters, activities, calendars, etc., is jam-packed with comics—the very same comics we'll be collecting in our graphic novels. The magazine is available wherever magazines are sold, and is also available as a subscription. Just go to Papercutz.com/nickmag for all the details.

Editors Michael Petranek and Suzannah Rowntree helped get the comics started, but the bulk of the editorial work was handled by Bethany Bryan (Associate Editor/Papercutz) and Joan Hilty (Comics Editor/Nickelodeon). Together, working with writer Stefan Petrucha, and artists Allison Stejlau and Mike Kazaleh, colorist Laurie E. Smith, and letterer Tom Orzechowski they've come up with the **BREADWINNERS** graphic novel you see before you.

But this is just the beginning! Coming up next will be the premiere **HARVEY BEAKS** graphic novel, followed by the second **SANJAY AND CRAIG** graphic novel, and then that's quickly followed by the debut of the first **PIG GOAT BANANA CRICKET** graphic novel! Is this the Nickelodeon Age of Graphic Novels or what? And the best part is that you are a BIG part of it! Tell us what you think of what we're doing—your opinion matters to us. Our goal is to produce graphic novels that you will love as much as the original TV shows. Write to us at the addresses below and tell us if we succeeded or not. We'll be waiting for your comments!

Thanks,

JIM

STAY IN TOUCH!

EMAIL: salicrup@papercutz.com
WEB: papercutz.com
TWITTER: @papercutzgn
FACEBOOK: PAPERCUTZGRAPHICNOVELS
FANMAIL: Papercutz, 160 Broadway, Suite 700, East Wing, New York, NY 10038

BUT THAT'S THE *WHOLE* IDEA, BAP!

ONCE WE GO ON SOME *WILD* RIDES...

...EAT SOME *BAD* FOOD...

...GO ON SOME *MORE* RIDES...

...AND EAT SOME *MORE* BAD FOOD...

YOU'LL BE TOO *EXHAUSTED* TO CARE ABOUT SILLY OLD CLOWNS!

YOU... REALLY... THINK... SO?

ZZZZZZZZZ

WHOA! YOU WERE *RIGHT!* I DIDN'T EVEN DREAM ABOUT CLOWNS!

HEY, WHY ARE WE SURROUNDED BY ALL THESE *GOOD-LOOKING* DUCKS?

I THINK WE FELL ASLEEP IN THE HOUSE OF MIRRORS!

HEY, SWAYSWAY? REMEMBER HOW MY BEING *EXHAUSTED* MADE ME NOT BE *AFRAID?*

YEAH, BAP?

I'M NOT TIRED ANYMORE!

PUNCH IT, BUHDEUCE!

BUT WE'RE *NOT* IN THE ROCKET VAN! WHAT DO I PUNCH? WHAT?

NEVER MIND! JUST *RUN!*

EASY, BUHDEUCE! WE'RE ALMOST AT THE PARKING LOT!

Y'KNOW, I THINK IT'S *LOCKED.*

LOCKED? WHY WOULD ANYONE *LOCK* A CARNIVAL AT *NIGHT*, AFTER IT'S *CLOSED?* I DON'T UNDER-STAND!

I DON'T *WANT* TO UNDER-STAND!

AT LEAST IT'S NOT A *CLOWN!* RIGHT?

SWAYSWAY? I SAID, AT LEAST IT'S NOT A *CLOWN!* RIGHT?

UH... BAP?

IT'S A CLOWN.

NO! NO! STAY BACK!

I NEVER SHOULD HAVE TAKEN THIS *STUPID* SECOND JOB AS A NIGHT WATCHMAN! THEY DON'T EVEN GIVE ME TIME TO CHANGE MY *CLOTHES!*

WATCHMAN? ⸢GASP!⸣

ALL THIS TIME I THOUGHT YOU WERE *EVIL,* A HEINOUS, LEERING BEAST-CLOWN!

BUT YOU'RE *NOT!* YOU'RE NOT THAT AT *ALL!*

BUT YOU'RE JUST SOME POOR GUY FORCED TO WORK A SECOND JOB AS A NIGHT WATCHMAN WHO PROBABLY THOUGHT WE WERE BURGLARS!

I DID! I DID! I THOUGHT YOU WERE *BURGLARS!*

⸢SOB!⸣ I'M... SORRY! HERE, TAKE MY MONEY!

CLOWNS, YOU ARE *FORGIVEN!*

I'LL NEVER BE AFRAID OF YOU AGAIN!

THANK-YOU! THANK-YOU!

SHAME WE DIDN'T NOTICE THIS *HOLE* IN THE FENCE EARLIER.

I LOVE CLOWNS! LET'S GO TO A CIRCUS!

I DUNNO, BAP.

SEEING HIM WHIMPER LIKE THAT WAS *REALLY* CREEPY! I NEVER REALIZED HOW *SCARY* A CLOWN COULD BE!

THE END

WHAT DID WE *DO?*

TELL US WHAT IT IS AND WE'LL *APOLOGIZE!*

A RARE PORTRAIT OF THE *BREAD MAKER,* DONE IN BREAD BY FAMED ARTIST *VINCENT VAN DOUGH,* WAS *STOLEN* FROM THE DUCKTOWN MUSEUM!

YOU TWO ARE *BREADWINNERS,* RIGHT?

YEP! TWO DUCKS WHO DELIVER BREAD IN A ROCKET-VAN!

WELL, WHAT IF YOU GOT *TIRED* OF DELIVERING BREAD AND DECIDED TO *PINCH* A LOAF FOR YOURSELVES? A LOAF OF *RARE PORTRAIT!*

WHO COULD GET *TIRED* OF BEING A BREADWINNER?

NO MATTER THE CHALLENGE, NO MATTER WHAT, WE ALWAYS DELIVER AND *NEVER* GIVE UP!

THERE'S NOTHING TO WORRY ABOUT, BAP! WE'RE *INNOCENT!*

AND IF WE'RE *INNOCENT,* WE'RE SAFE, RIGHT?

RIGHT?

DO YOU GET THE FEELING WE'RE BEING WATCHED, MY DUCKY-DUCK?

LIKE BY *MONSTERS?* NOT WITH THAT NICE LAMP HERE!

DID YOU BUY A *BUNCH* OF THE SAME LAMP ON SALE OR SOMETHING, BAP?

NOPE.

"HUH. THAT'S FUNNY.

"MAYBE *I* DID...

"...AND FORGOT."

THIS TIME, MAKE SURE YOU *FLUSH.*

SWAYSWAY?

YEAH, BAP?

BREAD Quarterly

WHAT DO YOU THINK WOULD HAPPEN IF WE CONFESSED TO STEALING THAT PORTRAIT EVEN IF WE *DIDN'T* DO IT?

DO YOU THINK THAT LAMP WOULD STOP *FOLLOWING* US?

I HONESTLY DON'T KNOW, BAP.

BREAD Quarterly

I'LL TELL YOU WHAT WOULD HAPPEN!

I'D READ YOU YOUR RIGHTS!

I'D HANDCUFF YOU AND TAKE YOU INTO CUSTODY!

I'D DRIVE YOU TO THE STATION!

WE'D DO A PERP WALK!

WE'D FINGERPRINT YOU!

THERE'D BE *FORMS* TO FILL OUT! *LOTS* OF FORMS!

A 22-A IN TRIPLICATE!

AN 86-R, BUT JUST ONE!

A 15-B IN DUPLICATE!

ANOTHER 22-A!

A 47-W! MY *FAVORITE!*

A 16-XYZ IN *PEN!*

A Z-6Z-Z...

ZZZZZZ

IT'S NOT LOST! IT NEVER LEFT!

WHOO-HOO!

WAIT. WHAT ARE WE TALKING ABOUT AGAIN?

THE PORTRAIT OF THE BREAD MAKER IS STILL *HERE*. IT JUST GOT SO *MOLDY* IT DIDN'T LOOK LIKE HIM ANYMORE, SO THEY RENAMED IT THE *MOLDY LISA!*

AND TO THINK, ALL I HAD TO DO WAS SWALLOW SOME *ROTTEN BREAD* AND GET *REALLY SICK* TO FIGURE IT OUT!

WAY TO GO, BAP!

WELL! I MAY HAVE MISJUDGED YOU TWO! GREAT WORK!

I'M STILL *TICKETING* YOU FOR SLOPPY PARKING, THOUGH!

BUTT...

NO BUTS!

OH, HE JUST LIKES SAYING BUTT.

BUTT, BUTT, BUTT, BUTT, BUTT...

THE END